Steven Seagull
Action Hero

VOTE CLAM

T. STARFISH

DETECTIVE
BEACH PD
S. SEAGULL

BEACH CITY PD

OXFORD
UNIVERSITY PRESS

Great Clarendon Street, Oxford OX2 6DP.
United Kingdom

Oxford University Press is a department of the University of Oxford.
It furthers the University's objective of excellence in research, scholarship,
and education by publishing worldwide. Oxford is a registered trade mark of
Oxford University Press in the UK and in certain other countries
Text and illustrations copyright © Elys Dolan 2016

The moral rights of the author and illustrator have been asserted
Database right Oxford University Press (maker)

First published in 2016

British Library Cataloguing in Publication Data
Data available

ISBN: 978-0-19-273869-1 (hardback)
ISBN: 978-0-19-273870-7 (paperback)
ISBN: 978-0-19-273871-4 (eBook)

10 9 8 7 6 5 4 3 2 1

Printed in China

Paper used in the production of this book is a natural, recyclable product made
from wood grown in sustainable forests. The manufacturing process
conforms to the environmental regulations of the country of origin.

SEAGULL·S
ENTRAPMENT

POLICE
MISCONDUCT

PECK!

DIRTY COP

For Steven Seagal and the Queen.
E.D.

THE SANDY TIMES
RENEGADE

STEVEN SEAGULL
KICKED OFF THE FORCE
Sergeant starfish revealed
today that well Known

Today Steven is retired.

But he used to be a cop.

Now Steven's ex-partner, Mac, needs him back on the force.

'I can't come back,' said Steven. 'Sergeant Starfish fired me for being too much of a renegade.'

'But we need you,' said Mac. 'Someone's been stealing Beach City's sand and leaving massive holes everywhere. Look, we're in one now.

Could Harry be a suspect?

'Harry, have you been digging these holes?' asked Steven.

'Nah, it wasn't me, guv,' said Harry. 'I've been too busy serving quality ice cream!'

ICE CREAM

Harry's

Now 100% Legit!

PUSH IT

All I wanted was an ice lolly!

'Yuck, this is definitely
Harry's ice cream,' said Mac.

Harry is innocent—this time.

Could Lola be a suspect?

'Lola, have you been stealing sand?' asked Steven.

'How dare you!' said Lola. 'I've been too busy saving people. Just ask Mr Davidson over there.'

Could Rick be a suspect?

'Rick, have you been digging massive holes?' asked Steven.

'I don't do that stuff anymore,' said Rick. 'Anyway, these holes have ruined our game!'

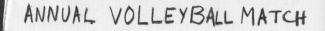

'Yep, Rick's game is in a whole lot of trouble,' said Mac.

Rick is reformed—for now.

Steven was stumped.
Who on Earth would need so much sand?

'Er, Steven?' said Mac.

IT'S CLAUDE VON CRAB! GASP!

'Ahoy, Steven!' said Claude. 'Finally, I have what every criminal mastermind needs. A base made entirely of sand!'

'Claude, I should have known that you were behind this,' said Steven. 'Come down with your claws up or I will fly up there and arrest you!'

'I'd like to see you try,' said Claude. 'We have beach balls and we're not afraid to use them. Show them, Big Tony!'

I bet they don't even have planning permission for that.

'Mac! Nooooooo!' cried Steven.

splish!

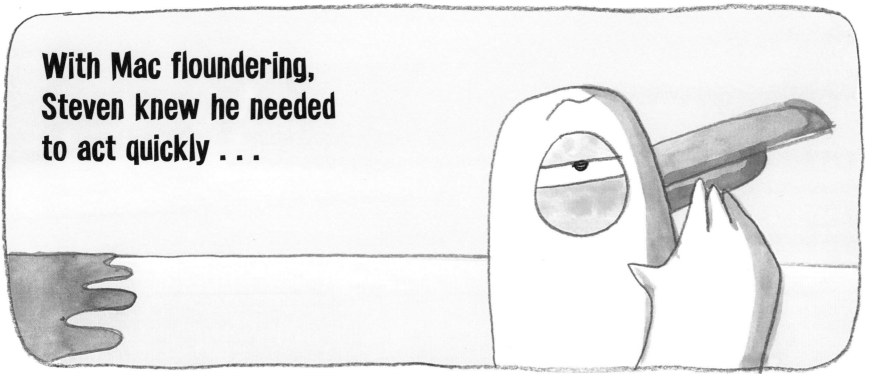

With Mac floundering,
Steven knew he needed
to act quickly . . .

'My friend is drowning!' cried Steven.

But Steven didn't seem to have much of a plan, until . . .

Everything became clear.

I don't like this plan.

Thanks to some quick thinking, Steven had conquered the castle and Beach City was saved.

Steven is back!